MURDER IN THE CIRCUS

VICTORIA MATTSEN CRIME SERIES
BOOK 3

IFEANYI ESIMAI

eISBN: 978-1-63589-793-7
Print ISBN: 978-1-63589-794-4
Audio ISBN - 978-1-63589-795-1

Get a FREE copy of The Rookie!

Join my Newsletter for updates, giveaways, teasers, and a FREE copy of the prequel - The Rookie. Click here or scan the QR code.

For Chinwe...Always.
The wind beneath my wings.

ACKNOWLEDGMENTS

My heartfelt gratitude goes out to my family and friends, whose unwavering faith in me fueled this project from the very start.

I also want to extend a special thanks to a group of incredible individuals whose generous spirit has made an indelible impact on this project, and for that, I am forever grateful.

Erik S
Nneka Anaebonam
Craig Martelle
Jenn Davidson
Chinwe Anyamele
Obioha Emezie
Renee
Okechukwu Obua
Romeo Richards
Ikenna Emeghara
Charles Onunkwo
Adaeze

Every one of you has helped shape this journey in your own unique way, and I couldn't be more thankful. Your support has not only made these books a reality but has also inspired me as I continue to tell Detective Vikki Mattsen's story.

To all the readers, thank you for inviting Detective Vikki

Mattsen into your lives. It's been a joy to share this adventure with you.

Here's to the stories yet to be told.

PROLOGUE

Schools were out for the summer—clowns, acrobats, jugglers, stunt performers, and elephants were in.

Retired ex-police officer Jon Jackson strolled toward the circus tent entrance dressed in his blue security uniform. It was a cushy job for a few nights—a different pace from working at the mall. Plus, fresh air.

He raised his head and drew in a deep breath. The circus brought out a nostalgic feeling in him. The smell of animals, manure, and hay reminded him of the farm he'd grown up on. He'd brought his grandkids here earlier in the evening. Now he patrolled the grounds, making sure everything was safe.

The circus performers parked their trailers about a hundred meters from the tent. Sudden bursts of laughter and conversations drifted from them. They would've patrolled the grounds themselves in the past instead of relaxing, but things had changed. They needed their rest. And he, the job.

The animals—elephants, horses, donkeys—grunted and snorted in their respective pens, one day of hard work behind them. Jon wondered if this was the last time the circus would come to town. The newer acts not using animals have risen in popularity over the years. The tickets were expensive, but the performances were out of this world—the costumes, displays, and ambiance at the venues were impressive. Traveling circuses like this one with performing animals, a holdover from the last century were teetering on extinction. People believed they were acting on borrowed time.

It wouldn't take much to deliver a death blow. One concerned community member whispering about *animal cruelty, or freeing the elephants,* and cancel culture reared its head.

Using big cats was long gone. It'd shifted indoors to Vegas, then declined. The only constants in the world are taxes, death, and change. Embrace change or die. But, if the circus continued to come every summer, he'd continue to attend.

Jon liked the trapeze show, especially the act with the blonde in the little red outfit. He chuckled. "Humans have learned to fly without wings."

He sighed, shifted the flap over the entrance to the tent, and stepped into the circular arena. A small yellow bulb worked hard, casting shadows across the tent. It never failed to amaze him how large it looked when empty. Tomorrow, excited children and their parents would fill the arena.

Ron Jackson walked from one end of the arena to the other. Last year he'd ejected a homeless man trespassing. He shined his flashlight across the empty seats, from one end of the tent to the other, to ensure the vagrant wasn't back with friends. Then he followed the beam up the tent wall and to the ceiling. He froze.

Was that a shadow? He brought his light back.

Jackson's pulse raced. He tilted his head and went closer.

"My God."

He fumbled for his cell phone in his pants pocket and tapped on the screen. When the phone rang, it was in sync with his heartbeat, pounding like a drum. He felt hot all over.

Sweat trickled down his back. He hoped he wasn't about to have a heart attack.

"Nine-one-one, what's your emergency?" a female voice said.

"H-hello, I'm calling from the big tent—"

"Where's that, sir? Are you injured?"

"No, no. I'm at the Dolittle Circus tent on the carnival grounds in St. Ives on Fulton Street. A woman—I think a performer—is hanging by her neck from a rope in the circus tent. I-I think she's dead."

CHAPTER ONE

St. Ives, a murder capital? That thought crossed Detective Vikki Mattsen's mind as she took in the flashing strobe lights of emergency vehicles outside the circus tent.

She parked her Ford Explorer close to a police cruiser but away from the big fire engine trucks—Rigs. To Vikki, they were mountains on wheels.

She'd dressed hastily after she'd got the call. Black pantsuit over a cream-colored blouse, she hoped she was presentable.

Vikki approached the yellow police tape perimeter at the entrance to the tent. A glance at her phone told her it was three a.m. Too early for onlookers to be hanging around to see what was happening.

She imagined the headline in tomorrow's newspapers. MURDER IN THE CIRCUS. Children and their parents would be disappointed tomorrow when the circus shuts down as investigations ensued.

"Detective Mattsen," said a uniform standing by the entrance. He tried to stifle a yawn but lost. "Sorry about that, ma'am."

He handed her a pen, then opened the crime scene logbook.

Vikki scribbled her name. "You don't have to apologize. It's early for me, too."

"Here you go." The uniform handed her a crime scene overall, CSO.

Vikki yawned and took it from him. This was her less favorite part of going to a crime scene—changing into protective overalls. She stepped into it, pulled it over her pantsuit, then covered her shoes with booties.

Vikki ducked under the yellow police tape and stepped into the circus tent. Her mouth dropped open. Even though it was a crime scene, inside a circus tent was always mesmerizing. The happier part of her childhood with Alexis and her family came to mind. Summer holidays like this included visits to the circus and all-you-can-eat hot dogs and cotton candy.

The fire service brought in searchlights, and the tent could've been a football stadium during the Super Bowl. Vikki's jaw dropped further when she saw the victim—a woman in red with a rope around her neck, hanging from the tent's ceiling.

They'd split open a side of the tent and extended a mechanical ladder from a rig toward the victim. Someone was up the ladder examining her.

Vikki shut her mouth when she noticed it was the medical examiner on the ladder, Dr. Ted Brandon, an acquaintance. He'd decided the take the job at St. Ives to be close to her, but she was not interested in a relationship. She saw her partner, Mike Gomez, approach from the corner of her eye.

"Mattsen! You can stop checking him out," Gomez said.

"Good morning to you, too. How did she get up there?"

Gomez shrugged. "That was the first thing out of my

mouth when I got here. But the ringmaster said they used a push-button lift to get that high. But it stopped working. Or you can climb. Which she often does as a trapeze artist."

"She did that to herself?" Vikki asked.

"I don't think so. We'll wait to hear from CSU and the ME. See what their take on it is. I think the ME's almost done."

Gomez walked closer to the fire service ladder Dr. Brandon was on. Vikki followed.

"Do we know who the victim is?"

Gomez glanced at a small notebook in his hands. "Eva Putikova, twenty-five. She's a gymnast...acrobat with the circus. A rising star."

"Who discovered her body?"

Gomez pointed at an older man in a private security uniform. "That's Jon Jackson. I got his statement. He's a retired officer with SIPD. He'd pulled the plug about three years ago. Ron was doing his rounds, shined his flashlight around in the tent, and discovered the body. He said he was here earlier with his grandchildren and saw her perform. He's still shaken."

Vikki and Gomez turned to a mechanical sound. The ladder with the ME was coming down.

Gomez nodded. "About time. Maybe he'll now have something to tell us concerning the time of death."

Vikki didn't want to give Dr. Brandon the impression she was waiting for him. She turned away. A man dressed in a long red coat approached. He could pass for Santa in another six months. His eyes darted from Vikki to Gomez, then settled on Vikki.

"Excuse me." He cocked his head. "Detective Victoria Mattsen?"

"Yes."

He let out a sigh like he'd been looking for her. "I'm Doug

Dolittle. I own the circus." His voice was hoarse and deep. The odor of cigar smoke hanging around him. He blew air out through his mouth and shook his head.

Vikki cocked her head. How did he get behind the yellow tape? The crime scene was contaminated.

"It's so tragic what happened here tonight. I remember when Eva started working for us, it was like yesterday. She was so full of life, full of promise." He produced a business card. "Please call if you have any questions. Also, you can pick up the videos of the show anytime if it will help get to the root of this."

Vikki took the card, surprised by his hello-and-goodbye approach. "Thank you, Mr. Dolittle. Did you hear anything tonight that could help with the investigation?"

"I slept like a baby. I took a sleeping pill. My wife woke me up when the police arrived."

Was he building up a defense wall?

Dolittle glanced around as if searching for someone.

"Did Eva have any enemies? Anyone who wanted to hurt her?" Vikki asked.

Mr. Dolittle's eyes widened. "But that seems like suicide. Do you think someone put her up there? I thought she did it to herself."

He turned and attempted to smile at a woman who joined him. Possibly his daughter. He said something to her.

Vikki shook her head. "We don't know yet. Did she show signs that might make you believe she did this to herself?"

"I can't say for sure," Mr. Dolittle said. "This is my wife, Kate. She knows more than I do about what's going on."

Vikki kept her face passive. Mrs. Dolittle, a fresh-faced blonde, about five feet eight with an hourglass figure, couldn't be over twenty-three. Mr. Dolittle robbed the cradle. "Hello, Kate. I'm Detective Mattsen."

Kate waved. "Hi, Detective. Everyone liked Eva. My

husband, Cowboy Jack, the clown, Morris Benson. The fortuneteller, even the elephants."

Gomez walked up to them. "Mattsen, the ME's ready for us." He nodded at Mr. and Mrs. Dolittle. "Good evening."

Vikki introduced them.

"I'm so sorry for your loss," Gomez said.

"Okay. I'll be right there." Vikki glanced around, saw a uniform, and motioned him over. "Please take Mr. and Mrs. Dolittle behind the yellow police line and get their statement."

The officer nodded.

"Detective." Mr. Dolittle stepped closer to Vikki and whispered, "This is a circus. The show must go on. You wouldn't shut us down. We have thousands of people coming. We don't want to disappoint them."

"We don't want to disrespect the memory of Ms. Putikova either," Vikki said. She fought hard to keep her composure. "Once we're done with our investigation, we'll release the tent to you. Please excuse me."

"This way, please," said the officer, shepherding the couple toward the exit.

Dr. Brandon smiled as Vikki approached. "Detective Mattsen."

Vikki nodded. "Dr. Brandon."

Gomez rolled his eyes. "Someone watching might think you two just met."

"Crime never sleeps, even in Joyland," Dr. Brandon said.

Vikki raised an eyebrow. "So, it's a homicide?"

"Yes," said Dr. Brandon. "The marks are obvious. If you hang yourself, the marks on the neck will angle upwards."

"The pull from the rope, right?" Gomez said.

Dr. Brandon nodded. "That's correct. And across if strangled from behind. This woman has both."

Vikki exhaled through her mouth. "So, the perp strangled the vic and then hung her to suggest suicide."

Gomez shook his head. "Jesus. Do you have a time of death?"

"Based on body temperature and lividity, I'll place the time of death between ten p.m. and one a.m." Dr. Brandon raised an evidence bag with three strands of long, straw-colored hair.

Vikki reached for the bag. Their fingers touched. It was pure electricity. She maintained a poker face and passed the bag to Gomez.

"Where did they come from?" Gomez asked.

"From her outfit," said Dr. Brandon. "Could be hair or something synthetic. I'll tell you more about them when I put it under the microscope." He held up another evidence bag.

Vikki did a double take. Heat rushed to her cheeks.

No way.

Dr. Brandon held up an engagement ring.

CHAPTER TWO

"Anyone presented one of these to you before?" Dr. Brandon asked. He didn't wait for an answer. "I found this in the victim's throat."

Vikki paused and fought the urge to slap him. But then, he didn't know about Bruce. She pushed it to the back of her mind and focused on the job at hand. She'd seen many crime scenes, but this was the first with an engagement ring inside the victim. How did it get into the victim's throat? Had she swallowed it by mistake? Had it been shoved down?

"I know you have many questions," said Dr. Brandon. "I'll have more answers after I bring her back to the lab."

"Thank you," Vikki said. Their eyes met. She pulled away and turned to Gomez. "We'll have to notify her next of kin. Did you find anyone?"

Gomez nodded toward an older woman sitting by herself. "That's the victim's grandmother."

Vikki walked over to her, introduced herself, and said, "I'm so sorry for your loss."

"My heart hurts," said the old woman in accented English.

Russian or from one of the former Soviet bloc countries, thought Vikki.

"What about Eva's parents?" Gomez asked.

"Drugs—drugs took them. Now, my Eva is gone, too." She turned to Vikki. "Eva never kill herself. Please, make who did this to her pay." The older woman touched Vikki's hand and squeezed. "Please do not let my granddaughter's death be unavenged. Eva *work* hard. She was going to leave this circus. She has agent."

Vikki returned the squeeze. "We'll do our best. Is there anyone you think wanted to hurt Eva?"

"No, but talk to Johnny."

Vikki narrowed her eyes. "Who's Johnny?"

"Johnny...Johnny, her agent."

Vikki brought out her notebook. "What's his last name?"

Eva's grandmother waved her hand in the air as if trying to shake the name off the tip of her tongue. Then she pointed. "Johnny."

A young man dressed in a blue blazer over a white shirt and blue jeans approached. Beads of sweat dotted his bald head. Vikki watched him. He was probably six feet tall, about two hundred pounds, with an athletic build. How did he get past the uniform outside?

"Johnny, Johnny!" the older woman said, her hand raised toward him.

The ME and his crew wheeled the gurney with a black body bag past them.

The man, Johnny, stared at the gurney as the medical examiner's technician wheeled it away. "Oh God, it's true." His voice broke. He covered his mouth with a shaky hand and paused to compose himself.

Vikki walked over to him. "I'm Detective Mattsen—my partner, Detective Gomez. What's your name, sir?"

"John Ronton. Eva is—was—my client." He touched Eva's

grandmother on the shoulder, said something, and then sat beside her.

"I never knew the circus used agents," Gomez said.

Vikki glanced at the agent. She was dying to hear the answer to that.

"If you want to be part of circus three-point-zero," John Ronton said. "This," he raised his hand and dropped it on his lap, "is the past. The new circus, the future, is what entertainment companies like Cirque du Soleil sell. They want only the best performers and can only take so many. Like traditional publishing, you need an agent who believes in your work to introduce you to publishers. Works with you to clean it up before presenting you to publishers."

Vikki nodded. "How did you become Eva's agent?"

"I saw her perform six months ago in Florida—noticed her potential right away. She was a natural. I met her after the show and tried to tell her how amazing she was." He laughed. "She blew me off. Called me a snake-oil peddler."

"What happened next?" Gomez asked.

"I wandered around the carnival. Saw the fortuneteller's booth and stepped in. Before she started, I told her about the gymnast and all the good things I could do for her. Could she alter my fortune to include success with the gymnast? She read my palms, then told me to return to the girl."

Gomez waved his hand dismissively. "Then Eva changed her mind?"

He nodded. "Yes. I didn't know it then, but the fortuneteller was her grandmother."

Vikki glanced at the older woman sitting, grieving quietly, then back to the agent.

"I paid for singing lessons, gymnastic sessions, self-help seminars. She was at the cusp of landing an amazing deal." He stopped and shook his head. "After all the work she'd put in, she kills herself."

Gomez shook his head. "No, she didn't. Someone did that to her."

His eyes went wild. Vikki feared they'd pop out of their sockets.

"Murder?" he whispered. He covered his face with his hands, bent over, and sobbed.

Vikki gave him some time. People grieved differently.

John Ronton sniffed and wiped his nose with the back of his hand. "Sorry... Please, please find who did this."

Gomez pursed his lips and said, "Is there anyone you think disliked Eva?"

"Everyone loved Eva."

Vikki rephrased the question. "Anyone competing with her? You said that the opportunities are few."

John let a beat pass, then shook his head. "I don't think she'd go that far. There's this girl, Sofia Hardly. She's good, too. When scouts come here searching for new prospects, they zero in on Eva and Sofia."

"You think this girl Sofia could do something like this?" Gomez asked.

John inhaled, then exhaled. "This is a cutthroat business. Competition is fierce. Eva's closest rival is Sofia. The other day, I saw Eva in the changing room, crying. She said Sofia bragged that the number two company after Cirque du Soleil was in talks with her. I told her not to worry. Her turn was coming."

"Was anyone in talks with Eva? About to recruit her?"

John shook his head. "Not that I know of."

Vikki wrote the name in her notebook. Now to rule out the agent. "Mr. Ronton, where were you between ten p.m. and one a.m. last night?"

CHAPTER THREE

The following day, Vikki arrived at the PD by seven-thirty a.m. This day was one of the few times she's gotten to the office before Jody Allison, the police department admin.

Once settled, she sent uniforms to pick up Sofia Hardly at the Good Road Motel. "It's going to be a rude awakening for her," Vikki muttered.

Gomez said he was bringing coffee. She pondered what to make of John Ronton and the previous night's interview.

When Vikki had asked him about his whereabouts, he had been apprehensive. John Ronton had only relaxed after she'd said it was a routine question they asked. He'd said he'd left after Eva's performance at nine p.m. and returned to his motel by Uber. He'd ordered room service, ate, and watched a movie.

Vikki had asked him which movie.

"*Die Hard*," he'd said.

Vikki had checked on Netflix. *Die Hard* was one of the top ten movies in the US today.

After the movie, he'd changed and was about to sleep when he got a text from Mr. Dolittle. He'd said it sounded like Eva had done something terrible. He'd dressed and returned to the circus, where he'd met them.

She pulled out of her reverie when Gomez arrived.

He carried a tray from Dunkin' with two cups of coffee and two paper bags wedged between the cups. Vikki hoped they contained donuts, not croissants stuffed with eggs, sausage, and cheese.

"Here we go." Gomez placed them on her table. "Are they here yet?"

"I don't think so," Vikki said. "No one has called me." The smell of bacon and eggs wafted up. She sighed and reached into the bag without grease stains, and her reward was a glazed donut. "Good choice." She took a bite and promised herself not to make it a habit. She finished the sweet treat and chased it down with coffee.

"Sniff, sniff. What's that awful smell?" said a familiar voice.

Vikki's insides tightened.

McClane bellowed, "Perhaps something the cat dragged in early this morning to foul up our mood."

Detective Sean McClane's taunts shouldn't get to her, but sometimes they slipped through occasionally.

Vikki boiled with rage. She and McClane had a history. An incident had occurred when Vikki was a rookie, and McClane was a field training officer. He'd touched her inappropriately, and she'd retaliated. It hadn't ended well for him. Many years later, they'd ended up at SIPD, and he made life miserable for her any chance he got.

Gomez drew in a deep breath and started to his feet.

Vikki shook her head. She didn't want to become an outcast among her colleagues. Nor to be treated differently because she was a woman. In this era of 'Me Too,' an official complaint from her could go all the way to the top, and disciplinary action against McClane, swift.

A uniform by the door caught her eye and signaled they were ready for her.

On her way out, Vikki approached McClane and said, "There a brown smudge on the seat of your pants. You may want to double-check if you wiped thoroughly. Maybe that's what you're smelling."

"Huh?" McClane said and began looking frantically over his shoulder, trying to see his back.

"I think it's on the other side," Gomez said, walking past him.

Vikki stood before the one-way window to interview room one and watched Sofia Hardly. She'd pulled her blonde hair into a ponytail and looked tiny in an oversized man's blue button-down shirt over faded blue jeans.

She appeared calm, but her eyes and the clenching and unclenching of her jaw muscles told a different story. Vikki wondered if she was looking at a killer.

Vikki knocked once and stepped in. "Sofia Hardly, I'm Detective Mattsen. My partner, Detective Gomez. How—"

"Why am I here?" Her voice was steady. She sounded like a child singing Christmas a cappella in church.

"I'll get to that if you let me," Vikki said. "You work at the Dolittle Circus?"

"Yes, but not for long."

Gomez raised an eyebrow. "Why do you say that?"

Sofia Hardly smiled, showing a gap tooth. "Because I have options."

"Okay," Vikki said, nodding. "Do you know Eva Putikova?"

Sofia drew back. "What?"

"Am I here because of the bitch? Little Ms. Goody Two-Shoes. She walks around as if her shit doesn't stink. But deep down—she's a sewer herself. Do you know what she did to me?"

Vikki was taken aback. Such venom. She thought it was a rhetorical question and said nothing.

Sofia repeated herself, her voice rising. "Do you?"

"No!" Gomez said.

The veins in Sofia's neck stood out. "She stole my boyfriend, then dumped him after screwing him. What was I supposed to do with him? Pick him up, dust him off, and continue where we stopped? Pretend it never happened?"

Never interrupt someone providing information of their own free will. Vikki didn't have to try. She was too stunned to speak.

"I loved John, and Eva knew that. She's downright mean. Has a beating rock for a heart." Sofia's chest rose and fell. She exhaled noisily through her nose. "One of these days, I'll wrap that trapeze rope around her neck and string her up like the fat pig she is."

CHAPTER FOUR

Vikki and Gomez exchanged glances.

Sofia's gaze bounced from one detective to the other.

The tension in the room felt like someone was holding a fart, and not sure if diarrhea or gas would leak when they let go.

Gomez smiled. "You don't like that girl?"

Sofia threw out her hands and relaxed into her chair. "What's there to like about her?"

Vikki cocked her head. "Okay, so last night, you made good on that threat. It was time you put her in her place. After the show, you lured her back into the tent after everyone was gone. Pretending you wanted to rehearse a new move, you wrapped the rope around her neck and strung her up."

Sofia's forehead furrowed. "What? No, you're crazy. I'd never—" She stopped and stared at the two detectives. "Something happened?"

"Last night, a security guard found Eva Putikova hanging in the circus tent," Gomez said.

Sofia raised an eyebrow and cocked her head. "Hanging?"

"Sofia, Eva is dead. Someone strung her up by her neck in the circus tent late last night."

Sofia jerked back. "Oh my God...oh my God."

"Where were you between ten p.m. and one a.m.?" Vikki asked.

Sofia's hand flew to her chest. "Me? What? Do you think I killed her? We have our differences, but murder?"

The news of the murder shook Sofia, Vikki thought. She appeared to be fighting back the tears. But it could be an act. "So, where were you last night?"

"Despite our enmity, we still needed each other to survive. Before the show ended, Sofia told me she wanted to practice a move. I stayed back until the tent was empty, and we practiced. After that, I left."

"What was the time, then?" Vikki asked.

"Maybe like nine or nine-thirty. I didn't kill her. By the time I left the tent, Eva was alive."

"Did anyone see you?" Gomez asked.

"I don't know. My boyfriend was already there. He'd waited for me to finish with Eva."

"Did anyone else see you and your boyfriend leave the circus after the rehearsal?"

Tears streamed down Sofia's cheeks. "I told you, I don't know."

"Think, Sofia," Vikki said. "You were the last person seen with her alive, and you had a reason to be mad at her. You said yourself you'd like to do this very thing to her."

Sofia frowned. "My boyfriend was hungry. We stopped at McDonald's. The drive-thru, then we went home."

"Home?" Gomez asked.

"It's a motel, Good Road Motel. We stay in motels when we're on the road. You know, like the one your officer pulled me from before I showered this morning." Sofia's head jerked up. "The receptionist at the motel. We'd engaged in small talk with him."

They'd let Sofia go after telling her not to skip town. Vikki returned to her desk, flopped into her chair, and turned the computer on. Gomez was on the phone already.

Moments later, Gomez sighed and hung up. "That was the motel. The night receptionist confirmed chatting with the couple last night. He said we're free to look at their CCTV feed. He'll send it by email."

"So, we have nothing," Vikki said.

"It seems like the circus ghost killed her."

Vikki raised an eyebrow. "Circus ghost?"

"Yep, every circus has a ghost haunting the crew. That's what Serena said when I got the call in the middle of the night about the murder."

Serena was Gomez's wife. Maybe she was half asleep when she said that.

"Mattsen! Gomez."

Vikki looked up. Captain Levin approached them. She got to her feet. Usually, he invited them into his office.

"Good morning, sir."

"Morning, you two. I heard there was trouble at the circus. Any leads?"

"Not yet, sir," Vikki said. "We're still working on it."

Captain Levin casually brushed off his suit. "The kids are out of school for the summer. They need a place to burn all that energy and keep out of trouble. Sort this out fast. An engaged child means happy parents."

Vikki knew the captain would follow up by saying the mayor had complained about the city's coffers and not wanting revenue to drop because a murder upset the apple cart. Instead, the captain surprised her.

"I'll be in my office. Think of the children."

Gomez turned to Vikki once the captain returned to his

office and smiled. "He said nothing about the mayor this time."

"Yes, maybe the mayor hasn't called yet." Vikki's phone rang. "Mattsen," she answered.

"Hi, this is Ted...Dr. Brandon. I have something to show you about the victim from the circus."

Vikki froze. After what had happened to Bruce, her TO (training officer), when she was a rookie, Vikki had stopped believing in love. To protect her heart, she only indulged in one-night stands. She'd met Dr. Brandon at a bar. He'd been on a temporary assignment. Things had worked fine until he'd taken a job with her employer, making them colleagues. Now her heart was getting involved.

"Detective Mattsen? Are you there?"

"Yes, I'm here. We'll be down in ten minutes."

CHAPTER FIVE

Vikki headed to the ME's office and felt like she was back in high school on her way to see a guy she'd crushed on. Vikki's relationship with Ted had started in reverse. She'd slept with him first before getting to know him. Who built a relationship like that?

Did that mean he cared about her? Most men worked hard to get the goods. And once they'd tasted it, it was bye-bye. She'd served herself on a platter. Now he wanted to hang around. Precisely what she didn't like. Vikki sighed. She couldn't win.

Gomez returned to the circus to get the performance videos. Maybe if he were with her, she'd be calm.

She entered the ME's office building and made her way to the morgue.

The odor of embalming chemicals assaulted her nose. That was one thing she'd never get used to. She grabbed the disposable gear from the shelf and put them on. Then she entered the morgue proper—always cold, always smelly.

Dr. Brandon stood in his blue scrubs and protective overalls, waiting for her. On the autopsy table was Eva Putikova. She looked peaceful.

Her body was naked, unmarked, but for the bruising around her neck. The thought that one day she'd end up on a table like this crossed Vikki's mind. She pushed the idea away.

Dr. Brandon glanced over her shoulder as if searching for someone. "Hi Vikki. Where's Gomez?"

Vikki took note that he'd called her Vikki, not Detective Mattsen. "He returned to the circus to get the security camera videos."

"The owner agreed to provide it?"

Vikki nodded.

"Most circus owners don't want any videos of the performances circulating online to ensure people come in person to watch."

"You're right, but he's eager for the crime to be solved quickly. They want to make the most of the season." Vikki spread her lips in a forced smile. "So, what do you have for me?"

Dr. Brandon pulled a pair of gloves from a box and slipped them on as he walked to the table. He waved a finger over Eva's lips. "There's bruising here." He parted her lips with his fingers, revealing more bruising on her gums. "I recovered a small tooth fragment in her mouth."

"She fought the person?"

Dr. Brandon nodded. "I think the attacker tried to shove the ring into her mouth and chipped Eva's tooth. The sharp edge scratched the person's finger."

Vikki's pulse picked up a notch. "You think we can get DNA from her mouth?"

"I hope so. I swabbed her mouth and lips and sent the samples to the lab. We'll keep our fingers crossed."

Vikki relaxed, a warm feeling spreading in her stomach.

She liked the guy but was restraining herself, following self-imposed rules that had worked in the past but were now coming apart.

Dr. Brandon walked over to a table with a microscope. He picked up a remote control and clicked it. A flat-screen TV mounted on the wall came on. "Remember those fibers I showed you at the scene?"

"Yes. There were three of them." On the screen was a microscopic view of hair strands.

"In human hair, the color and pigmentation are fairly constant throughout the length of the strand. In animal hair, the color changes are apparent at brief intervals." He clicked and moved the screen forward. "So, what we have are animal strands."

Vikki raised an eyebrow. "What else?"

Dr. Brandon chuckled. "That's it until we get back the DNA result from the mouth swab."

Vikki tucked her chin. She forced a smile to hide her disappointment. But thirty minutes earlier, she had nothing.

"However, watch out for any clothing with animal fur. The wearer is a person of interest to talk to as you investigate the case."

Their eyes met. She turned away.

Ted clasped his gloved hands together. "Do you want to talk about whatever happened in the past? What about getting together for a drink or two later in the evening?"

Vikki wanted to, but the job came first. "I'll take a rain check." It wasn't a complete dismissal. "Once Gomez returns, we'll have a ton of video footage to wade through. Thanks, though."

She turned and walked away and sensed his gaze lingering on her back. At the dressing area, she took off and trashed the protective garb.

Strolling back to her desk, her mind kept on drifting to

Ted. The corners of his eyes crinkled when he smiled. She was in trouble.

CHAPTER SIX

Gomez was back in the office when Vikki returned. He'd brought back with him five hours of video. They divided them into two. One focused on the actual performances and the other on the security camera.

"So, what did Ted say at the morgue?"

Vikki briefed him, excluding the part about meeting up for drinks. She didn't need to be teased relentlessly.

Gomez pulled his eyes away from the screen. "That's interesting. If the DNA recovered from her mouth matches one in the CODIS database, we'll have someone to focus on at least."

Gomez returned to the screen. They continued in silence, each to their thoughts. Then Gomez broke the silence.

"I was talking to Serena about you and Dr. Brandon," Gomez said. "And—"

"You what?" Vikki couldn't understand why people stuck their noses into other people's businesses.

Gomez grinned. "Hold your horses. Serena thinks the world of you. She believes you're punishing yourself unjustly."

Vikki's gaze bounced between Gomez and the screen.

Gomez continued talking and smiling. He was distracting her.

"Why don't we talk about this later, so we can focus and not need to go through these videos again."

"We won't miss anything," Gomez said. "You guys have a made-in-Heaven relationship, and there's no need to fight it. The guy has fallen for you. And I think you like him."

Vikki pantomimed, jabbing two fingers at her eyes and pointing at his computer screen. "Gomez, you'll miss something important."

He turned to the screen. "No, it's fine. It's just some parents taking pictures with flashes and the ushers telling them not to. The flash distracts the performers." He growled, shaking his head. "Some parents have a thick skull. She's at it again."

They went for a few more minutes without Gomez saying anything. Those videos must be more entertaining for Gomez. For Vikki, monitoring people as they walked in and out of the tent was like watching paint dry.

"The show is not bad at all," Gomez said. "What a shame what happened to Eva. Seeing them perform together, I could see what Sofia was talking about. They needed each other for a flawless performance."

Vikki paused her video and leaned over to see Gomez's screen. She watched them performing together. "Wow, they're talented."

"Confident and skillful," Gomez said. "Their execution is perfect. Anyway, Mattsen, just in case Serena and I run into you anywhere, she'll ask you if I delivered her message about Dr. Brandon."

"No, she won't."

"Yes, she will. Just remember to say yes. Mike gave me your message."

Vikki laughed. "I will."

For the next thirty minutes, they focused on the monotonous work.

"Excuse me, Detective Mattsen?" said a voice.

Vikki looked up. It was Santiago. She smiled. "What's up?"

"I checked the motel. The receptionist confirmed Sofia and her boyfriend returned around nine-thirty. They stayed in and didn't go out again. They have CCTV in the lobby to prove it if we want it."

"Thanks, Maria. I'll add that to her note. Those videos can be a pain to watch. Let's hope we won't need to go through them, too." She didn't want to tell her they'd already confirmed that and discourage her.

Maria left, and Vikki continued, eyes glued to the screen. Her eyes fluttered, then she heard snoring. Beside her, Gomez's chin dipped. A snore rattled out of him. Vikki's eyes flew open. She elbowed him.

"Mike, Mike, wake up," Vikki whispered.

Gomez awoke with a jerk. He swiped his hand across his face and refocused on the screen.

"Look at that. I didn't know they had a cowboy act, too," Gomez said, not missing a beat, pretending he was never asleep. He just asked Eva to be his partner. He's going to lasso her."

Vikki saw the arena fill up and empty twice. People gathered in front of the tent as the show time approached. Then the show began, and folks moved in to get seated. The reverse happened when the show ended.

What about the staff? None of them came through the front. The elephant she wouldn't have missed. "Is the tent's back entrance as wide as the front? I wonder if they have a camera covering it." From her periphery, she noticed Gomez lean closer to his screen.

"Mattsen, come see this."

CHAPTER SEVEN

Vikki paused her video and focused on Gomez's screen. He was rewinding his video.

"Now watch. Focus on the cowboy. I think he's called Texas Jake."

The man, Texas Jake, dressed as a cowboy, sauntered into the circle. He ambled around, dancing and swinging his lasso. Vikki tried to figure out what the act was. He was only waving a rope in the air. Anyone could do that. Maybe maintaining the wide loop in the rope as he waved it around required finesse.

Then he introduced his partner, Eva. The crowd cheered. She was their favorite, too. Eva blindfolded Texas Jake, then walked to one end of the ring. A staff member spun Texas Jake around. In the meantime, Eva had changed position.

Vikki understood the game now. He'd lasso Eva despite being blindfolded and not knowing her location.

Texas Jack raised his hand and twirled the rope. He cocked his head a few times, then threw the rope and lassoed Eva. The crown applauded. He reeled her in like a fish. They hugged when they finally came in contact. Texas Jake watched her for a moment, then kissed her. Eva pushed him away.

"Did you see that?" Gomez asked.

"It seemed like Eva didn't want to be kissed. It wasn't part of the act."

"Yes, yes," Gomez said. "She didn't sign up for that. Don't forget the rope. He's good at knots. But look at his vest."

Vikki focused on Texas Jake's fancy vest with fur-like fringes. "It's the same color as the strands recovered from Eva's clothing." Was she looking into the face of Eva Putikova's murderer?

CHAPTER EIGHT

Vikki set up a murder board while Gomez and some uniforms went to pick up Jake Avery, aka Texas Jake the Cowboy, for questioning.

She turned to the sound of footsteps behind her. It was Captain Levin. She glanced at the wall clock opposite where she stood. It was after twelve.

"Mattsen, I heard you have a breakthrough with the investigation."

"Good afternoon, sir. We're still following up. A person of interest showed up on CCTV. We hope to learn more soon."

"Is he a member of the circus?"

Vikki nodded.

The captain wished her Godspeed and left.

Vikki's stomach rumbled. She contemplated grabbing something to eat from the deli next door. Or wait and go with Gomez. That might mean delaying the interview. Instead, she went to the vending machine and got a chocolate chip granola bar.

She'd just finished her snack when Gomez walked into the office.

"I got the vest and logged it with the forensic unit," Gomez said. "They'll get back to us soon. I could use some food before interviewing him. He's already in the interview room. I have a uniform standing by the door. He's not going anywhere. Let's eat and give Jake the Cowboy time to marinate."

They ate fast in the deli close to the PD. Vikki had a six-inch roast beef sub with sweet and hot peppers, American cheese, and spinach. Gomez, a one-foot Philly cheesesteak. He called it a man's meal. They returned to the PD and went straight to the interview room.

Texas Jake was twenty-six years old, six feet tall, and easily one hundred ninety to two hundred pounds. He looked like the boy next door.

"Hi, Jake. I'm Detective Mattsen. You've already met my partner, Detective Gomez."

Jake nodded. "I don't know why you brought me here. It's not gonna change nothing." His voice was calm with a Texas drawl. "I've already told Detective Gomez I had nothing to do with what happened to Eva."

"What happened to Eva?" Vikki asked.

Jake drew in a breath. He exhaled and leaned back. "She was found dead."

"Where were you between ten p.m. and one a.m. last night?" Vikki asked.

Before Jake could answer, someone knocked on the door. A CU investigator poked his head in.

"Detective Mattsen, so sorry to bother you. Do you have a moment?"

Vikki stepped out.

The investigator handed her a piece of paper and said, "The fibers from the crime scene and the suspect's clothing were a match."

"Thank you." Vikki read the report and smiled. Unless

Jake was Houdini, he wasn't escaping this one. She stood still, relishing the moment. All they needed was a confession from Texas Jake, and they could put this behind them. Vikki reentered the interview room.

Gomez raised an eyebrow.

"Jake, the fibers on your vest match those retrieved from Eva's clothing from last night. The rope used to hang her matched the one you use for your act." Vikki was reaching here. There was no mention of the rope. "Why don't you tell us what happened?"

"We know she rejected your advances," Gomez said, gesturing with his hands. "We saw you on video. Video images don't lie. You were mad. As soon as the tent cleared out and you two were alone, you tried to connect with her again. She rebuffed you again, and this time you lost your cool and strangled her."

Vikki waved the paper in the air. "You didn't mean to kill her. It was a crime of passion. So now you must cover it up. You cut out a rope from your lasso and made a knot. To make it appear to be suicide."

Texas Jake leaned forward. "Detective, you have an amazing imagination. Yes, I liked Eva. So did her agent, John Ronton. Old fart, Dolittle, Morris, and every other horny bastard who bought a ticket to see her. Are you investigating them, too?"

Gomez threw open his hands. "Jake, we're following evidence."

Jake shook his head. "Believe me. I had nothing to do with what happened to her. The fibers could have gotten on her during our performance. She was my partner. What if someone is intentionally trying to frame me? Did you think of that?"

Vikki had thought of that. But as Gomez said, they

followed leads. "So, where were you between ten p.m. and one a.m.?"

Jake opened his mouth, then closed it. He let out a breath.

"The evidence against you is damning," Vikki said. "If someone can verify where you were, this is your chance to bring it up."

Jake sighed and swore under his breath. "I was with Kate—Mrs. Dolittle."

"You were with her? How?" Gomez asked.

"We were together in my trailer knocking boots. When we saw the police lights, she returned to her trailer and woke up her husband."

Vikki exhaled. The euphoria she'd felt earlier evaporated.

CHAPTER NINE

Vikki returned to her desk.

Gomez was in his chair, dazed and oblivious to others in the squad room. He shook his head. "This is a roller coaster of a case. One moment it looks like it's going to get solved. The next, we're back to square one."

Vikki massaged her temple, trying to fend off a headache. They'd let Jake the Cowboy go with instructions not to leave town. To Confirm his alibi involved inviting Kate Dolittle to the police station. And that could undo her marriage if her husband found out. "I don't think we have a choice," Vikki muttered.

"Have a choice for what?" Gomez said.

"Sorry, it wasn't supposed to come out loud. I considered inviting Mrs. Dolittle over to hear her side of the story. But again, I don't want to upset her apple cart."

Gomez shrugged. "But that's not our concern. We have a murder to solve. When you decide to have an affair, you should be ready to accept the fallout."

Vikki sent uniforms to pick up Kate Dolittle, keeping her fingers crossed that her husband might not be home.

When Kate arrived, she had her husband in tow. Even though Vikki was all about taking responsibility, this stumped her.

Gomez suggested they separate them. He'd take Mr. Dolittle to interview room one. Vikki would question Kate in room two without jeopardizing her marriage.

But Mr. Dolittle insisted he stayed with his wife during the interview when Vikki suggested it.

"I see what you guys are trying to do," said Mr. Dolittle. "You want to separate me from my wife? I already know about Jake and Morris."

Vikki tried to keep her face passive.

Mr. Dolittle fixed his gaze on Gomez. "Detective, as you age, all you need is companionship."

Gomez cleared his throat and pulled at the lapel of his suit. "Really."

Vikki tapped a finger on the table. "Okay. That gets a few pressing concerns out of the way. Now, who is Morris again?"

"Morris Benson? He's the circus clown," said Mr. Dolittle. "I haven't seen him since last night." He turned to his wife. "Sweetie, did you...?"

She shook her head.

"He used to see Kate regularly until about two weeks ago. Then he called it off."

Gomez cocked his head. "And how did you know?"

"Because I watch from behind the curtain," Dolittle said. "They pretend they don't know I'm there."

Vikki swallowed. "Why did he call it off, Kate?"

"I'm not sure," Kate said. "But I think it had something to do with Eva. He wanted to save himself all for her."

Vikki nodded as the picture came into focus, like a Polaroid photo. A bizarre arrangement that worked had unraveled when Morris had called it off.

Kate Dolittle collaborated with Jake's alibi that they had been together while her husband was asleep.

After they left, Vikki suggested to Gomez that they watch the videos again. "Maybe I missed something, or you missed something."

"I missed nothing, and I focused on the screen. Didn't I find Jake's vest?"

Vikki didn't want to argue too much. She was tired. "Dude, you fell asleep. Be a good sport. Let's give it a second go."

This time around, Vikki sped up the video. She was on the lookout for the clown. After ten minutes, she turned to Gomez. "Did you see any clowns when you watched the performance?"

"Of course. It's a circus!"

Vikki shook her head. "I'm telling you, I have seen none for the past ten minutes."

Gomez paused his screen and watched with her for five minutes. "It seems like something happened to the clown."

Vikki reached into her pants pocket, pulled out the business card from Dr. Dolittle earlier that morning, and called him. He answered on the third ring.

"Mr. Dolittle, Detective Mattsen here."

"Detective, did we forget something?"

"No, I have a question. In the video we're reviewing, the clown wasn't there. You have a clown, right?"

"Yes. His name is Morris Benson. He's the circus clown, not a figure of speech. You can't call yourself a circus without a clown. He was there, I'm sure. Maybe you haven't seen him yet." Mr. Dolittle chuckled. "He has a short fuse. Tell him what he doesn't like, and he gets in your face. What was that, honey?"

In the background, Mrs. Dolittle spoke to her husband.

"Kate says he's very possessive, too. Thinking back, she thinks he was angry with Eva."

The tiny hairs on the back of Vikki's neck rose.

"When was the last time either of you saw him?" Vikki asked.

Mr. Dolittle repeated the question out loud.

"For me, I don't remember. But Kate saw him at the circus during Jake's act. When Jake was doing the rope thing."

"During the cowboy act?" Vikki asked.

"Yes."

"Does she remember anything else?"

Again, Dolittle repeated the question.

"Nope, but if she does, I'll call you. Detective, we need to sort this out. I can't afford to remain closed for another day. The show must go on."

"One more thing before you go. Where can I find Morris?"

"He has a trailer on the grounds. The one with 'clown' written in large print. You can't miss it."

"Thank you." Vikki hung up.

Gomez's gaze was on her, the detective hungry for information.

Vikki rewound the video to the beginning of Jake's act. "Morris Benson is a person of interest. He's the clown, but I didn't see him in the video. I learned from Dolittle and his wife that he has a short fuse and was angry with Eva that day."

"Oh?"

"Kate said she last saw him during Jake's act. I'll take another look."

"I did a thorough job watching the video. But have at it anyway if you think there's still a needle in that haystack."

Vikki went for it. She watched the video. Then she saw the clown after Jake lassoed Eva, pulled her in, and kissed her.

He was off to the side by the grandstands, easily missed. She could tell the clown was no longer happy despite the makeup.

Vikki remembered what Kate Dolittle had said. He could be possessive. "Gomez, let's go talk to Morris Benson."

Gomez was sitting with his legs on his desk and his attention on the screen. All that was missing was popcorn. "Why don't we have a uniform bring him in?"

"No, there's no time. I wish we'd focused on him earlier. He could be anywhere by now."

CHAPTER TEN

Vikki drove to the circus with Gomez riding shotgun. The circus looked different during the day. Darkness and light in the right combination always result in beauty. Now, it was just light.

Finding Mr. Benson's trailer wasn't difficult. The giant clown text printed on it stood out like a beacon. Vikki prayed he was home. Talking to him would shed light on what had been going on.

She got out of the car and approached the trailer. She smelled them before she saw them—animal manure and fresh hay. About twenty-five meters to her right, two elephants stood close to their trailer, stuffing hay into their mouths with their trunks while basking in the sun.

"Jesus, those things are huge," Gomez said. "You think they'll charge us?"

Vikki's mouth went dry. She swallowed and touched the butt of her Glock. "I-I don't think so. As long as we mind our business, I believe they'll mind theirs."

"I see them on TV in the Serengeti. When they're pissed,

their ears flap like butterfly wings, with their trunks in the air."

"I think these are Asian elephants. Most elephants used by circuses are the smaller and easier to manage Asian species."

Vikki climbed the small stairs that led to the trailer, happy to get out of sight of the gentle giants. She took a deep breath and knocked on the door. "Morris Benson, SIPD. Open up!"

She waited a moment, then banged on the door louder. "Mr. Morris Benson, this is the police. Open up. We want to ask you a few questions."

Silence.

"We're coming in, and we're armed."

Vikki tried the doorknob. To her surprise, it turned. She pushed the door in and hoped that was enough Exigent Circumstances. She removed her Glock from the holster and held it in a two-handed grip, the nozzle pointing down.

She walked in cautiously. Gomez was behind her, his weapon drawn.

The odor of a two-day-old kitchen garbage smell was unmistakable.

Gomez groaned. "We need an open window here."

Vikki said nothing but continued to examine the trailer. It was one open space with a bed in one corner, unmade. An old, brown leather couch occupied one wall. A small sink and a counter with a hotplate made up the kitchen.

There was a table and chair stuffed next to the couch. On the table were a few books. Vikki recognized a Robert Dugoni hardback, Stephen King's *The Stand*, and a James Patterson paperback.

There were two framed pictures on the table. One was with a group of circus performers. Vikki recognized Jake the Cowboy, Mr. Dolittle, his wife in the group, the elephant she'd seen outside, and some people from the video she'd watched earlier. The clown was there, with his face painted. What was his normal appearance without the clown paint?

She picked up the other framed photo. A young man with black hair and thick eyelashes with protruding ears. She turned to Gomez. "Do you know what Morris Benson looks like?"

"I guess that's him in that frame."

Vikki Googled the circus on her phone and went to the 'About' page. She found Mr. Benson. Same guy in the frame. She raised her phone. "It's him."

"Of course it's him. I wouldn't put a picture of someone else on my table." He paused. "Maybe, depends on who."

Vikki chuckled and leafed through the novel, *The Stand*.

"I don't think he's been here in the past few days," Gomez said. He walked to a small door and opened it. "Closet. Where's the toilet?"

"It's called outhouse or Porta-Potty," Vikki said. "It should be somewhere outside."

Gomez shook his head. "Imagine waking up in the middle of the night to take a leak, and you have to go outside? Even in winter."

A piece of paper in the novel caught Vikki's eye. She took it out and scanned the text to see if it was anything they could use. Nothing. "I don't want to imagine anything like—"

Vikki stopped talking. The piece of paper was a receipt, and it was for an engagement ring.

CHAPTER ELEVEN

Vikki's pulse raced. The date on the receipt was a few days ago.

Gomez walked over. "What's that?"

"A receipt for an engagement ring. Purchased two towns over at Milton Mall." She took a picture with her phone, fished out an evidence bag from her pocket, and dropped it in. She handed the evidence to Gomez.

Gomez's breath caught. "We should call the store and find out who bought it and when."

Vikki shook her head. "I think we should log it in at the station, then go there in person."

Thirty minutes later, they were driving on the back roads to Milton.

Vikki raised an eyebrow. "What do you think happened?"

"Who knows? Maybe he proposed, but the chick said no. He got mad and choked her to death. Crime of passion, simple."

They arrived at the mall. Vikki drove around for a few minutes before they found parking.

"All these people who come to malls on weekdays, don't they have jobs?"

"They'll be wondering the same about us," Vikki said. "Remember, it's summer, too. Some people take time off."

Vikki consulted the map of the mall's ground floor and found the store's location. When they walked in, about three couples were in the store. Two were being assisted while one peered at the rings on display.

A blonde, probably in her late twenties, dressed in a black skirt suit and a million-dollar smile, walked up to them and said, "I'm Mary. Welcome to Royal Jewelry. Is this your first time coming to our store?"

Vikki nodded. She knew what came next. It had happened when they had investigated the drowning at St. Ives Lake.

"Are you shopping for an anniversary ring?"

Vikki flashed her badge. "No, but we'll like to know about an engagement ring purchased here two days ago."

Mary's smile wavered. "Why? What happened?"

"We're investigating a homicide," Gomez said. "We have the receipt and want to know who bought it."

The color drained from Mary's face. Her fingers flew to a gold crucifix pendant on her necklace. "Come—come this way." She led them to a computer terminal that was not in use. "Can I have the receipt, please?"

Vikki showed her the receipt on her phone.

Mary glanced at it. "Anna rang up that sale. But she's off today."

Gomez exhaled. "Is there a way to get to her as soon as possible?"

Vikki's heart sank. They were so close, yet so far. She scanned the store. There were probably hundreds of thousands of dollars worth of inventory here. "Can we see your security videos from two days ago?"

Mary hesitated. "Can... Can I see your badges again?"

Gomez smiled. "You can never be too careful. Has someone robbed your store before?"

Mary nodded.

Vikki exhaled. "Why don't you Google SIPD? You'll find our pictures there."

Mary did just that. She walked over to another computer and typed. After a few clicks of the mouse, she glanced at Vikki, then the screen. She did the same with Gomez. The worry lines on her face faded.

"Come with me." Mary led them through a door that said *STORE PERSONNEL ONLY. DO NOT ENTER.*

They walked down a dark corridor and stopped at a closet without a door. A computer monitor hung on the wall. Wires connected it to a blinking console on the floor. The screen showed different scenes from inside the store and outside. Another monitor was blank on a table.

Mary pulled out the drawer on the table, and a keyboard appeared. She typed on the screen, and the blank monitor came to life.

"The time on the receipt was sixteen twenty-five, last Saturday...terminal two. I'll back it up a minute." She hit enter. An image of the computer terminal appeared on the screen.

Vikki's pulse picked up a notch—the moment of truth. When you were waiting for something, a minute became an eternity. Soon, a figure approached the screen. Vikki held her breath.

"That's Morris Benson," Gomez said breathlessly. "Can you make us a copy, please?"

"Sure," Mary said. She opened another drawer filled with promotional items. Mouse pads, letter openers, and a thumb drive all had The Royal Jewelry logo. She picked up a thumb drive and inserted it into the USB drive.

"We have to find Mr. Benson," said Vikki.

Gomez nodded. "But where?"

"Someone must know something. Maybe there's somewhere else he hangs out," Vikki said.

Mary handed the thumb drive to Gomez.

He smiled at her. "Thank you."

Back in the car, Vikki had the engine running while they brainstormed. They concluded that the first thing was to locate Mr. Benson.

"We have to put out a BOLO on Morris Benson," Vikki said. She picked up her cell phone from the dash. "I'll call Mr. Dolittle again and find out what car Morris drives and any ideas about where he could be."

Gomez opened the door and stepped out. "I'll call the department and have them look at his DMV record and send us what they have." Gomez shut the door, leaned against the car, and brought out his phone.

Vikki's call to Dolittle lasted less than two minutes. Just as she hung up, Gomez opened the car door and stepped inside.

"Morris Benson drives a white 2015 Ford F150. They've put out a BOLO," Gomez said.

"Exactly what Dolittle said. Morris also has a room at Sunshine Motel in St. Ives." Vikki engaged the car's gear. "St. Ives Motel, here we come."

CHAPTER TWELVE

Vikki joined the evening rush. What would have been a thirty-minute drive on Route 80 turned into a sixty-minute stop-and-go. Her right leg ached by the time they pulled into the motel.

The parking lot was almost full. There were trucks, a few eighteen-wheelers, and one or two luxury sedans. It seemed like it catered to transients and people who paid by the hour.

She saw a space near a dumpster, took it, and killed the engine.

Gomez let out a breath, opened the door, and stepped car. "Mr. Benson better be here."

Gomez met Vikki by the trunk. His shoulders dropped. He was ready to call it a day. Then his eyes came alive. "Wait a minute." Gomez pointed at the car next to Vikki's. "Isn't that the car we have a BOLO for?"

Vikki glanced at it. "What do you know?" By chance, they'd parked beside Benson's car. "Well, at least we know he's here."

They entered the lobby, and Vikki flashed her badge at the South Asian man at the reception desk. His thick white beard and Malcolm X style glasses seemed out of place on his face. "Do you have a Morris Benson here?"

Gomez showed him a picture of Morris on the circus's website on his phone.

The man glanced at the phone, then his forehead furrowed.

Gomez could tell the man recognized the picture. "Which room is he in?"

The receptionist nodded. "I think we have him. He's on the ground floor, down this corridor." He pointed to his left. "Room eleven."

"Is he in the room right now?" Vikki asked, noticing that the man had no accent. She'd expected one.

"I haven't seen him today. Normally, he crosses the lobby to get to his car. There's an exit at the other end of the building. He could've left from there, too."

"Thank you," Vikki said.

They headed for room eleven.

When they got there, Gomez knocked on the door. "Morris Benson! SIPD, open the door!"

Vikki listened. No sound came from inside initially. A faint rustle of papers reached her ears. She made eye contact with Gomez. He cocked his head. He'd heard it, too.

Vikki slapped her open palm on the door three times. "Morris Benson, this is the police. Open the door!"

No answer.

She turned the doorknob. Locked. The rustling sound came again.

"Someone's in there," Gomez.

Vikki banged with her fist. "We know you're in there. This is the police. Open the door!"

Nothing.

Vikki turned to the sound of approaching footsteps. It was the guy from reception.

"I have a key."

"Unlock it and step aside," Gomez said. He removed his Glock from his shoulder holster.

The man unlocked the door and moved away.

Vikki pulled her gun and held it in a double-hand grip. She nudged the door with her foot. The door creaked open, followed by the rustling sound again. Someone was in there.

Vikki's pulse raced. "Police officers! We're coming in, and we're armed!" She pushed the door open.

CHAPTER THIRTEEN

The door swung open. It was a standard motel room—a chair, table, flat-screen TV, and a queen-size bed with rumpled sheets. A closet and a slightly open door led into the bathroom.

"Morris Benson, this is the police. Show yourself," Vikki said.

Nothing.

Gomez indicated he was going to check the bathroom. Vikki nodded. Once he'd cleared the toilet, the closet was next.

Gomez nudged the door and peered in. "Clear."

A loud swishing sound rose behind Vikki. Her stomach all but dropped to the floor. How could she be so careless? She whirled, finger tightened on her Glock's trigger, a few pressure points from discharging a bullet.

There was nobody behind her. It was an oscillating table fan, ruffling the pages of a *Circus* magazine. Next to the magazine was a bottle of Courvoisier and two glasses. Vikki licked her dry lips. She could do with a drink now.

A closer look at the magazine showed that the images were mainly of Eva Putikova in different poses, with the caption: Up-and-Coming Aerialist.

A picture of what was going on took shape in Vikki's mind. Eva had been about to move on to the next stage of her career, and not everybody was happy about it.

A creak of the floorboards behind her caught her attention. She turned to face a closet. Was someone in there? She held her breath, listening for any other sounds.

Vikki grabbed the handle with her left hand. She made eye contact with Gomez. He gave a nod and leveled his gun at the closet door.

Vikki turned the knob and pulled. It felt heavy in her hand and opened slowly. She stepped back, her gun held in a double grip, heart hammering.

The body of Morris Benson hung on the door, reminding Vikki of a beef carcass in a cold room abattoir. His hands were bound in front of him in a handcuff knot with a necktie.

Vikki stumbled back. "DB." Her voice was a whisper.

Gomez was on his radio. "We have a dead body." He rattled out the motel's address.

It took about fifteen minutes for the ME and additional uniforms to arrive at the scene. The CSU technicians wasted no time dusting for prints. Uniforms knocked on neighbors' doors, asking if they'd heard or seen anything.

Dr. Brandon photographed and examined the body while it was still hanging. He recovered a typed suicide note from the breast pocket.

Vikki snapped on gloves, took the note, and read it aloud.

She said no to me. She rejected my ring. I can't go on living without her. Morris Benson.

Vikki put the note in a plastic bag. The lab would search for fingerprints and DNA. Next, she inspected the rope and the improvised handcuff. It looked too simple—like staged. Vikki let out a breath. "I don't know what to make of this."

Gomez tapped a finger against his lips. "What about he went to where she was rehearsing in the big tent and proposed? We already know he has a temper. She said no, so he strangled her. To direct suspicion away from him, he used Jake the Cowboy's rope to hang her."

"I see where you're going with that," Vikki said. "Morris comes back to his room, remorseful and regretful. Death is permanent. At least he can join her. He creates a noose from bedsheets and a handcuff knot from his tie. He puts the noose over his head and tightens the knot on his hand with his teeth. He drowns himself in Courvoisier, dulling his reflexes—climbs on a stool, kicks it away, and hangs."

Gomez shrugged. "So even if he changes his mind, his hands are tied. Excuse the pun. Before he can rescue himself, he's asphyxiated."

The shutter sound of the medical examiner's camera continued in the background. Vikki turned around, scanning the room. There was no coffee table about—another hole in her theory.

Dr. Brandon finished taking his pictures. With the help of two assistants, he removed the body from the closet door and placed him in a body bag. He let out a sigh and turned to Vikki and Gomez. "Detectives, the picture you painted is plausible. But there's one problem. Like last night's victim, the strangling came before the hanging. He was already dead before he was hung. Body temperature and lividity place the time of death between midnight and two a.m." He pointed out the marks on Morris Benson's neck.

"Probably the same perp," Vikki said.

Dr. Brandon nodded, then pointed at the bottle of brandy. "Morris Benson had probably been drinking when the killer confronted him. He's a big man. He would have fought hard. Life will always defend itself. His reflexes must have been slow if it was a full bottle, and he did that much damage to it. I'll order a full toxicology report once I get him to the lab."

CHAPTER FOURTEEN

Vikki wanted to go home, but the unsolved homicides beckoned. Instead, she drove back to the police station with Gomez riding in the passenger side.

They entered the squad room and headed straight for their desks.

Her cell phone rang as soon as she sat.

"I wouldn't answer that," Gomez said.

Vikki sighed. Too tired to check who it was, she said, "Mattsen."

"Detective, is it true my clown is dead?"

Vikki recognized Mr. Dolittle's voice. "I'm afraid so. We found him at the motel." She didn't give more information.

"Oh God, I'm doomed," Mr. Dolittle said. "We'd planned a rehearsal tonight for Eva's memorial at the big tent, and Morris is dead, too." He paused. "But this is show business. The living must continue living. The show must go on."

Vikki had other things on her mind. "Mr. Dolittle, the police have released the tent. You can use it as you please. The current crime scene is at the motel. The show can go on.

But please don't leave town if we need more info from you. I have to go." She hung up before Dolittle could get a word in.

Gomez raised an eyebrow. "The cuckold gentleman?"

Vikki nodded. "Yes."

"I'll grab some coffee from the break room. You want anything?"

Vikki blew air out through her mouth. "Before you go, hear me out first. See if this makes sense." She gestured with her hands. "So, let's say the victim, Morris Benson, is dating Eva and sleeping with Kate, his boss's wife."

Gomez raised his hand. "And the boss doesn't mind—because that's motive right there."

Vikki nodded. "And the boss doesn't mind. Then two days ago, Morris Benson buys an engagement ring and calls it off with Kate. Then someone kills Eva with her engagement ring not on her finger but in her throat. Because Morris called off their affair, Kate could have done it out of jealousy. But she has a strong alibi. Physically, I don't see her carrying it out." She paused for effect. "A few hours later, Morris is murdered, same MO as Eva." She glanced up at Gomez. "Does it make sense so far?"

"Mattsen, it's a bizarre case. What about Eva rejecting him? She said no to the engagement because she found out he was cheating. Morris gets emotional and kills her. Then staged it as a suicide. He goes home, is remorseful, and kills himself."

"But remember, Dr. Brandon said the perp strangled Morris first and then hung him," Vikki said. "They made the homicide look like a suicide similar to Eva's."

Gomez nodded. "Listen, my brain is bogged down. I need coffee to clear it up. If we go by what you're saying, the killer is still trying to cover their tracks." He stared into space and said, "St. Ives Strangler. I'm sure your friend Angie would like that title for her article. Let me get some coffee. Maybe that will help me think better."

"Get me one, too."

Gomez tapped his pocket and frowned. "What the...?" He dug his hand in and brought out a thumb drive. "Oh." He tossed it to Vikki.

Vikki caught it. "The CCTV footage from Royal Jewelry?"

Gomez nodded. "Why don't you take a second look? Maybe we overlooked something." He walked away, grinning.

"*Touché*," Vikki said and smiled. She turned her computer on and plugged the thumb drive into the USB port. She fast-forwarded the video and started watching before Morris Benson paid for the ring.

Vikki noticed a man in a blue jacket and Yankees baseball cap. He kept pulling his hat down as if trying to hide his face. After Morris Benson paid and walked away, the man followed.

The phone on Vikki's table rang. She sighed, paused the video, and picked it up. "Mattsen."

"This is Dr. Brandon. I'm glad I caught you. We got a match with the DNA from Eva's mouth."

Vikki needed clarification. "Which DNA?"

"Remember the chipped tooth scratching the perp's skin."

"Yes!"

He told her.

"Maybe there was a reason it was there. We'll follow up on it tomorrow. Thanks," Vikki said and hung up.

She clicked play and continued with the footage. The man followed Morris Benson out. Who was he? Vikki hoped the camera got a better shot of him somewhere. As the man stepped through the door, he raised his head and looked at the. "Bingo."

Vikki froze. The tiny hairs on the back of her neck stood like metal spikes. She rewound the video and froze it when the man glanced up.

She recognized the face. Eva Putikova and Morris Benson's murderer stared back at her.

Everything came together. They'd been looking in the wrong place.

CHAPTER FIFTEEN

Vikki stood inside the circus tent, her gaze at the center of the ring. She'd entered through the side entrance meant for the performers only. Adrenaline coursed through her system.

The searchlight focused on the man talking on the platform. He was handsome, solidly built, and held the microphone with sausage-like fingers. It was a sad gathering of all the circus members but two.

"Yesterday was a day of sorrow at Dolittle Circus. We lost a shining star—Eva Putikova. I had the privilege of working closely with her. Eva was beautiful inside and out. She was very dear to me—"

Vikki took a step forward. "So, why did you kill her?"

The staff members gasped.

John Ronton whirled and faced her. "What? Mattsen!" His eyes widened.

Vikki walked toward him. "After the show last night, she told you she was engaged. She was going to accept an offer from another circus with her fiancé. She told you that her contract with you was over."

The man made a halfhearted attempt to smile. "What—What are you talking about?"

"Eva thought you'd be happy for her. She trusted you and turned her back on you to continue her practice. You grabbed her from behind and squeezed the life out of her. But you didn't stop there."

He stepped back as Vikki got closer. "I didn't kill anybody."

"Then you had a better idea—murder-suicide. You strung her up and staged her death as a suicide. Then you went to her fiancé's motel and murdered him in cold blood. John Ronton, you killed Morris Benson."

Another gasp came from the circus members.

Ronton whirled and ran.

"Stop!" Vikki yelled.

The man ran a few more steps, then stopped. He walked back toward Vikki, his hands in the air.

Coming toward him were Gomez and three uniforms. Their guns pointed at him.

Vikki unclipped her cuffs. "John Ronton, you're under arrest for the murder of Eva Putikova and Morris Benson. Anything you say can and will be used against you in court." She cuffed him and read to him the rest of his Miranda rights. She handed him over to the uniforms. "Please take this piece of garbage out of here."

CHAPTER SIXTEEN

Vikki and Gomez sat in Captain Levin's office opposite him. It was dark outside. She would have been up for twenty-four hours in the next few hours.

Captain Levin smiled and raised his hands. "Congratulations, Detective Mattsen. It was..."

Gomez went into a violent coughing fit.

"Jesus, Mike! I was going to get to you, too."

"Sorry, sir. Something went down the wrong pipe."

"Yeah, yeah, I was born at night, but not last night. Great job to you, too, Detective Gomez. That is what I call teamwork. Mattsen, how did you get him to confess?"

Vikki glanced at Gomez. He gave her a nod. "They found his DNA in tissue extracted under both victims' nails and Eva's mouth. His hands showed scratch marks, probably when the victims fought for their lives. He knew the game was up."

Captain Levin raised his hand, then let it drop. "Sometimes, I don't understand people's actions. What was his motive? Not that there could be a reason for what he did."

"You're right, sir," Gomez said. "His last three clients fell through. Then he met Eva and sank everything he had into her—different training. I think he fell in love with her, too. She was his ticket to success and love. Then one day, Eva told him Mr. Benson had proposed to her, and they were signing with another circus. He wouldn't sit idly and watch his investment walk away."

Vikki nodded. "Right. Ronton planned to get rid of Morris so he couldn't propose to her. That's how he got into the video camera at the jewelry store. Whatever he planned didn't work, and Morris bought the ring." Vikki stifled a yawn. "Yesterday evening, after Sofia left, Ronton came to see Eva while she was practicing. She must have told him about the engagement and showed him the ring. According to Ronton, 'I lost it.' Within seconds, the deed was done. Eva was dead. Strangled. Ronton forced the engagement ring down her throat. He used the lift the circus used to hoist her up."

"Part of his alibi was he'd take an Uber from Eva's to the Motel at nine p.m. How did he fake his Uber ride?" Captain Levin asked.

Vikki pursed her lips, then said, "Only one ride back to his hotel was real. He ordered room service, booked the movie, and off he went. He tricked Morris—told him he came to congratulate him on his engagement."

"I'm guessing," Gomez said, "Morris dropped his guard and drank more than he normally did in the spirit of reconciliation and celebration. Then John Ronton surprised him."

"Exactly," Vikki said. She made a show of stretching and yawning, then stood. "I have to run, sir. It's been a hectic day and night."

"Same for me," said Gomez, getting up. "The wife is outside waiting for me."

"Well done again. See you two when I see you."

Outside the captain's door, Gomez turned to Vikki. "You

look tired. Serena can drop you off, too. I'm sleeping off once I get in the car."

"Phew. I'm tired, but I'd chase bad guys for another twelve hours if need be. Don't worry about me."

"If you say so. Goodnight." Gomez hurried off through the door and vanished into the night.

Vikki exhaled and walked back to her desk. She was tired but wouldn't leave without tidying her table. She got to her desk and froze.

A black man in scrubs was in her chair, sleeping. His bald head rested on his thick arms folded on her table. He snored softly.

Vikki's eyes scanned the squad room. It was empty, but faint voices drifted in from the corridor. She ogled him, thinking of what if's, a faint smile dancing on her lips. Why was she being hard on herself?

Her eyes must have a smoldering effect because Dr. Brandon inhaled deeply and let it out in a rush through his nose. Without warning, his eyes flickered open. "Hey, Vikki... Detective Mattsen."

Vikki frowned. "Dr. Brandon, what are you doing here?"

He sat up, rubbed his palm down his face, and stretched. "I heard about the arrest, and I came to congratulate you and drop off the autopsy finding for your report." He tapped a folder beside him on her desk.

"You shouldn't have bothered. I'd have picked it up in the morning." Her gaze darted to the folder at her table. "Anyway, I have to go."

He got up and towered over her five feet eight inches. She felt safe in his presence.

"I'll drive behind you to make sure you get home safely."

"You don't have to." She chuckled and pointed at herself. "You get me home safely. Who's going to make sure you get home safely?"

"I'll take my chances."

Vikki shrugged, picked up the folder, and headed for the door. Outside, she got into her Ford Explorer. All the notion of sleep was gone from her head. She started her car and watched him get into his rented vehicle. She engaged the gear and drove out of the parking lot. His lights came, and he was right behind her.

Why was she so hard on herself? She remembered what Serena had told Gomez. Her gaze darted from the road to the rearview mirror to make he was behind her. She kept within the speed limit, signaling before she took any turn.

The closer they got to her place, the more her resolve dissolved. Her heartbeat was out of control. A fire started in her stomach and spread all over her body. She had some wine —invite him in for a nightcap. Yes, that should do the trick, and see what developed.

Her pulse raced as the entrance to her apartment complex loomed. She slowed, signaled, then turned in. Her gaze never left her rearview mirror. One horn tap later, and Dr. Brandon's car drove past and continued down the street. Vikki shut her eyes tight, slowly shaking her head.

ABOUT THE AUTHOR

Ifeanyi Esimai is a mystery and crime writer and enjoys reading across different genres. When he's not writing or reading, he's exploring documentaries on museums and ancient history.

Click here or the image to get all ten books!

Get a FREE copy of The Rookie!

Join my reader group for updates, giveaways, teasers, and a FREE copy of the prequel - The Rookie. Click here or scan the QR code

Prologue

Jessica Reid felt like the entrée. The eyes of the man she loved were on her. She sat in a booth at Peachebees Restaurant—giddy, happy, and relieved. She wore a white and blue tie-dye summer dress with an off-shoulder design. Her long, golden hair cascaded down to her shoulders, resembling a waterfall.

The smell of well-done steak reached her nose. The

culprit was a smoking platter carried by a waiter walking by. Her mouth flooded with saliva. Maybe that's what she should have ordered instead of a chicken Caesar salad.

At thirty-two, her body wasn't the calorie burner it used to be at nineteen. Now she needed another set of eyes to monitor things she shouldn't be eating.

Jessica took a sip from her glass. The liquid cooled her inside on its way down. She loved Pinot Grigio for her dinner. It never failed to smooth the way for after-dinner activities. She couldn't wait to relax after hosting a couple on their honeymoon at her home that doubled as a bed-and-breakfast.

She batted her eyes at Vince, sitting opposite her. He smiled back. His eyes said it all, slicing through all the noise —laughter, conversation, and cutlery clanking on dinnerware. He loved her.

Their gazes locked, their eyes piercing into each other's souls. His eyes resembled the vast blue sky, and she eagerly anticipated losing herself in their depths once they returned to her house.

His manly dinner of potatoes and steak came. He didn't start eating until her Caesar salad arrived. They focused on their plates, comfortable in the silence, only loud between people not in tune with each other.

For dessert, they both got Irish coffee.

"I hardly saw the couple," Jessica said. "I thought they would be out and about. Do touristy things like hike on the Stairway to Heaven in Vernon, for that panoramic view."

Vince nodded. "Or visit Lake Mohawk in Sparta. Take a stroll on the boardwalk while enjoying their favorite ice cream."

Jessica snapped her finger and thumb repeatedly as if it would aid her memory. "Or visit the Stirling Museum at Ogdensburg to see all those glowing gems." She thought of her ten-year-old son, Rick, and her smile widened. "Rick can't get enough of the place. Did you know that parts of the movie *Zoolander*—the one with Ben Stiller—were shot in that mine?"

Smiling, he shook his head.

Jessica knew he was humoring her, and she loved him for that. Because she owned a bed-and-breakfast in St. Ives, Sussex County, she had to be ready with tourist ideas for her guests. People came from everywhere for that holiday experience that wouldn't break the bank.

The couple had rented the whole bed-and-breakfast section of her house for the weekend. But they rarely left the room.

"Why're you smiling?"

"The couple I just saw off at the train station would have saved a lot by renting a hotel room instead."

Vince took her hand, raised it to his lips, and kissed it. "Who knows? Maybe they did it for the experience."

His hot breath bathed the back of her hand, and heat coursed through her.

He raised his eyebrows. "So, they were on their honeymoon?"

Jessica beamed. "And they seemed genuinely in love." She chuckled and lowered her eyes. "Of course they should."

Vince massaged her hand. Then he said, "When will you give me an answer?"

Jessica's inside tightened. The smile on her face faded. Why did he have to go there?

"Marry me, Jessica." He choked with emotion.

She pulled her hand back and turned away. "Vince, I've told you—I'm not ready."

"That's not good enough, Jess. When will you be ready?"

She sighed. "I don't think I ever will. You know why." She grabbed her handbag from the table. "Why don't you leave well enough alone?" She opened her purse, peeled out five twenties, and tossed them on the table. "Bye."

Jessica headed for the exit. She knew people were watching but didn't care. She'd had enough. This had to end.

The blonde receptionist smiled as she approached. She glanced over Jessica's shoulder, and her smile wavered.

"Yeah, do what you do best—run away!" Vince said, following her. He had almost caught up with her. "You always think you're better than everyone. This time, I'll deal with you."

His words tore through Jessica. Her heart could've been a tomato tossed into a blender and shredded. She yanked the door open and walked into the warm evening.

Jessica wasn't sure where she parked her red BMW X5. She had her thumb on her car's fob keyless entry and pushed it repeatedly. Her car winked—she headed for it.

Vince's ranting got louder and closer. Her skin burned as if she were on fire. She increased her pace.

Jessica got into her car and started the engine. She lowered her window, fixed her gaze on him, and laughed sarcastically. "So, this would have been my reality if I'd agreed to marry you. Thank God for little mercies. We are through!"

Vince froze. His face turned white. He shook his head from side to side. "No, no."

"Yes, we are!"

Vince's facial features hardened. He could've been sitting on the ceramic throne, trying to squeeze one out. The veins on his neck became electric cables. His lips quivered. Without warning, he lunged forward.

Jessica floored it.

He grabbed the door, but his hands slipped off. He raised his fist. "You'll pay for this—bitch!"

Chapter 1

Jessica called her friend Sally to tell her she was almost home, and to bring Rick back.

She drove into her driveway at 7:30 p.m. and pushed the button to open her garage—then changed her mind. Better that she parked in the driveway so Sally would know she was home.

For the past two hours, she'd driven around St. Ives, the event at dinner going over and over in her head. Vince's image in her rearview mirror was etched on her mind.

How did a romantic dinner, on track to end with passion, crash and burn?

It was a mutually beneficial relationship. Good company. Sex on demand. Steady-flowing two-way traffic—symbiotic. Most men would kill for that type of arrangement. But not Vince. He wanted more. But she'd always been clear.

Been there, done that, and got the scars—no marriage for her.

Had she overreacted?

Was something else...[Click here for Dead in the Mansion]